Achilles the Donkey

ACHILLES THE DONKEY

by

H. E. Bates

Illustrated by Carol Barker

The donkey's mother always reminded him, "You are not called Achilles for nothing. If you're ever in trouble, run." Famine came to the rocky valley in Greece where Achilles lived a good life and the farm was sold. He was sent by ship to a faraway island and a new master, and he was sea-sick all the way. Achilles became a real beast of burden — starved and overworked. One day in the market place where he stood with six baskets of food on his back in the broiling sun — a pelican brought him onions and carrots and told Achilles to REBEL — to take his mother's advice and RUN! There was no stopping Achilles and he was a beast of burden no more.

K

Classification and Dewey Decimal: Easy (E)

About the Author:

Born in England, H. E. BATES has gained an international reputation as a novelist, short story writer and essayist. His work has been translated into many languages. He is an inveterate traveler and always comes home with an intensified love for England. His chief recreation used to be fishing and cricket, both of which he has given up for lack of time and now confines himself to gardening and writing. He champions young and unknown authors. Mr. Bates has never limited his writing to any one idea or theme and he has recently turned to writing for children.

About the Illustrator:

CAROL BARKER, an English, fourth-generation artist, began her first sketch book when she was ten and has been sketching and drawing ever since. She spent one year working with her father who, as a painter and designer, influenced her more than anyone else with constructive criticism, often severe, but always giving new ideas and building high standards. A holiday in Greece inspired the Achilles stories, now a trilogy which have won international acclaim. Carol Baker is now married and her main ambition is to continue bringing up her two children, traveling and of course, to illustrate children's books.

Achilles the Donkey

ACHILLES

THE

DONKEY

by

H. E. BATES

&

CAROL BARKER

1966 FIRST CADMUS EDITION
THIS SPECIAL EDITION IS PUBLISHED BY ARRANGEMENT WITH
THE PUBLISHERS OF THE REGULAR EDITION
FRANKLIN WATTS, INC.
BY
E. M. HALE AND COMPANY
EAU CLAIRE, WISCONSIN

This edition lithographed in U. S. A. by Wetzel Bros., Inc., Milwaukee 2, Wisconsin

When Achilles the Donkey was still very young and still very, very ignorant of what went on in the world his mother often used to talk to him in the stable where the two of them lived in a rocky valley in Greece, with a family of peasants, all among groves of olives, pines and fig-trees.

"Always remember," his mother used to say to him, "you are not called Achilles for nothing. Do you know who Achilles was?"

"No, mother."

"Achilles was a runner in ancient Greece. The fastest runner in the world in his day."

"Yes, mother."

"Your father was a good runner too. Not so fast as Achilles of course. But still pretty fast. And he always used to say that if ever a donkey got into trouble he could always get out of it if he could run fast enough. You understand?"

"Yes, mother."

"I suppose you know they call us beasts of burden?"

"Do they, mother?"

"They do, and your father didn't hold with that. He said we donkeys had a long and proud history. We shouldn't let ourselves be put upon, he said. 'Bring the boy up to be a good runner,' he used to say, 'and all will be well.' You understand?"

"I think so, mother."

Up to the time when his ears were growing to full size and his voice hadn't quite broken Achilles found life very easy. Every day his mother took the farmer's wife on her back to the cornfield and Achilles trotted along behind. His food was plain but good and there was generally plenty of it. Mostly it was corn but sometimes one of the children gave him a fig. He had no complaints at all.

Then dreadful things began to happen. No rain fell in the valley for months and months and months and months. The sky was always fierce and hot and blue. The streams all dried up. The fields all turned to dust. The corn all died and even the fig-trees started to wither away.

Not only donkeys and other animals but peasants too hadn't

enough to eat and because of this the peasants soon had to make a terrible decision. They had to sell their farm.

And not only the farm. They had to sell hens, pigs, goats,

sheep, cows, donkeys and—of course, Achilles. Yes: Achilles had to be separated from his mother. Far away on the island of Mykonos the farmer had an elder brother who needed another donkey and so to Mykonos Achilles had to go.

"Always remember you're not called Achilles for nothing,"

his mother told him as she said good-bye. "Don't cry now. If you're ever in trouble run. Don't let them put upon you."

So Achilles, weeping big tears, began his long journey and

almost at once they began to put upon him. First they loaded him into a broken-down, bumpy old truck. He was walloped about everywhere. Then he was unloaded at a big, hot, dusty port called Piraeus. He stood for hours on the quayside, scorched by sun.

All over the port there were ships, green ships, red ships, white ships, blue ships, black ships, some going, some coming, some standing still, some blowing hooters, some crammed with

people. Achilles had never seen anything like it; he was absolutely bewildered; he simply didn't know where he was.

Then the time came, towards night, when they loaded him into one of these ships. It was all black and dirty and its name was *Moskanti*. It was ghastly. It smelt horribly of oil. Achilles hated it from the first and was terribly, terribly homesick for the smell of corn.

He was also very lonely. Although he was tied up by his halter with several other animals on deck, some cows, a few goats, a horse and a big tabby ship's cat, they were all strangers to him. He didn't know a soul.

Then the ship started to move out of the harbour, and soon to the open sea. Then the wind started to get up and the ship began rocking up and down. As darkness came on it got colder

too and Achilles and the other animals simply shivered like jellies where they stood.

Worse than all this, Achilles was sea-sick. He turned a peculiar green colour. He shut his eyes as tightly as he could and just wanted to die.

night

Then after hours and hours of this awful cold green nightmare he opened his eyes and saw that dawn was breaking. The ship was coming into a little harbour. There were white and blue and reddy-brown houses and on the quayside lots of people stood waving their hands.

When one of the ship's sailors at last led Achilles down the gangway his legs were still so wobbly that he could hardly walk. People were bustling about everywhere. He had never seen so many people. Sailors, porters, girls, priests, taxi-drivers, children, fruit sellers, ice-cream men, men on bicycles: there were so many of them he felt almost off his head.

And then out of all this crowd one man suddenly came towards him. He was a rather fat, squatty old man with enormous grey-white moustaches, rather surly black eyes and a big straw hat.

And all of a sudden, with a sinking heart, Achilles realized that this man was his new master.

Very soon he was being led away through little, old, narrow, cobbled streets. He was still very shaky after his sea-sickness and it didn't help very much when every now and then the man gave him a frightful bang with a big stick on his haunches.

"You're as stubborn as all the rest of them!" the man shouted. "I'll learn you! Get a move on, can't you?"

"I'd run if I could," Achilles thought and at the same time knew that his legs would never carry him.

And then at long last the man brought him to a halt. He found himself in a tiny dark stable and he knew he could smell another donkey.

"Come very far?" the other donkey said after a long silence. It sounded very old and tired.

"A terrible long way."

"My advice to you, my boy, is to get some rest while you can. You won't get much later on."

"No? I'm terribly hungry. Don't I get anything to eat?"

"Midday. Only one meal a day here."

Achilles had hardly had time for forty winks before the old man was back again. Now Achilles could smell fruit. Lots and lots of fruit: tomatoes, bananas, figs, apples, grapes, peaches. And vegetables too: onions, carrots, potatoes and so on.

The smell of all these things made him awfully hungry but he hardly had a moment to think about it before the man walloped a heavy wooden saddle on his back. This was about twice as heavy as anything he had ever carried in his life and on an empty stomach it was more than he could bear.

His knees wobbled like jelly.

"Stand still!" the man shouted and gave him an enormous staggering biff! with the flat of his hand.

Then the man started to load baskets of fruit and vegetables on to the saddle, fastening them with rope. First just two of them, and then four—and then six. It was awful and Achilles felt that each one of them weighed a ton.

"Get on with it now!" the man shouted and prodded Achilles with a big stick. "Look sharp!—off you go!"

Achilles could hardly stand up, let alone walk; but somehow he did walk. In a daze he plodded back through the little, old, narrow cobbled streets, his legs all of a quiver.

At last he was in a market place. Like the quayside it was full of people, bustling, talking and shouting. All the time the old man shouted "Bananas! Figs! Grapes! Potatoes!" and so on and all the time, for hours and hours, while Achilles stood quaking on his empty stomach in the boiling sun, people came to buy fruit and vegetables.

Next morning it was the same; and the next; and the next. With nothing but one miserable handful of maize and a drink of water at midday Achilles felt he was wasting away to nothing but skin and bone. He was absolutely in despair.

"I'd run if I could," he was always thinking, "but I know my legs would never carry me."

And then an extraordinary thing happened.

One morning in the market place Achilles opened his eyes and thought he saw a big fluffy pink cloud coming down on top of him. Then he saw that it wasn't a cloud. It was a bird: a

great pink bird with pink feet, pink eyes and a long pink beak with a yellow streak underneath.

It was a pelican; and in the most friendly way it came and sat down by Achilles and started talking.

"Hullo, young fellow," the pelican said, "how are things with you?"

Achilles hadn't the heart to tell him. He simply wagged his tired ears.

"Just got in from Africa," the pelican said. "Rather a long flight. Still, mustn't grumble. Went pretty well on the whole. Could do with a bit of good grub, though."

"Who couldn't?" Achilles said.

"Seems plenty here," the pelican said and pointed with his beak at the mounds and mounds of fruit and vegetables stacked about on all sides. "Some pretty nice fish too, I see. Makes my beak water."

"I daresay it does," Achilles said. "But that doesn't help *me* much."

"You sound a bit under the weather," the pelican said.

"A bit?" Achilles said. "Another day of this and I'll die."

"You mean you want to get out of here?"

"I'd give both my right legs," Achilles said. "I'd give anything. I'm at the end of my tether—and what a tether, I tell you."

For a moment the pelican didn't say anything; then it took

a quick look round the market place and suddenly whispered something in Achilles' ear.

"No?" Achilles said. "I can't believe it."

"Just be ready," the pelican said.

"I'll try," Achilles said. "But I don't think I've got the strength to do it. I'm starving."

"Don't be silly. Of course you can do it. I'll bring you some food," the pelican said. "Tonight."

That night, when it was dark, the pelican flew into the little stable with a bunch of onions and two large bunches of carrots. Achilles had never tasted anything like it; the carrots especially were delicious; he nearly wept with joy.

"This'll put the strength back into you," the pelican said. "This'll pep you up no end. Especially the onions. By the way, my name's Popo."

"I simply don't know how to thank you, Popo."

"You can thank me by doing just what I tell you. You understand? *When I give the signal—run!*"

Achilles didn't sleep much that night, mostly from sheer excitement but partly because the onions made his tummy rumble round a bit. But in the morning he felt quite all right again. He had saved a few of the carrot tops and two onions for his breakfast and these put a lot more pep into him, as the pelican had said they would.

Then, as usual, he plodded down to the market place, heavily loaded down with baskets, looking like a real beast of burden.

"But I'm not going to be a beast of burden," he kept thinking. "Not any longer. My father didn't hold with it and nor do I. I'm going to—REBEL!"

Most mornings he shut his eyes when the sun got hot but this morning he kept them wide open, watching for his friend Popo the pelican to appear.

And suddenly he saw him, sitting high up on a big bright blue sunshade put up over a fish-stall. As he saw his friend Popo sitting there Achilles' heart started beating very fast and it went faster and faster as he waited for the pelican to give the signal. And then at last the signal came—two flaps with the right wing and two flaps with the left—and the pelican flew into the air.

A moment later you might have thought an earthquake had hit the market place. Achilles jumped about two yards forward

and upward and then three yards upward and backward. He stood first on his forelegs and then on his back legs, doing a sort of see-saw. He bared his teeth and set his ears at a terrible angle and gave a colossal angry bray:

"Hee-haw! Hee-haw! Hee-haw—haah!"

Then he started running. Fruit and vegetables went flying up into the air. The half empty baskets on his back rocked madly from side to side. The old man waved his stick and shouted and bashed the air with his hat. Everybody else in the market started shouting too and two old ladies at the fish-stall screamed like anything as Achilles went racing by.

"Stop him! Stop him!" the old man yelled. "Stop him! He's

gone raving mad! He gets too much good food! That's what! Stop him!"

But there was no stopping Achilles now. He was all steamed up like an express train. He ran at a terrific speed. All the time he could see his friend Popo the pelican flying ahead, leading the way, and he knew that all he had to do was to follow him.

Soon he was racing along a hot white country road. Some distance ahead of him Popo was sitting on the roadside, waiting.

"Whoa! there," the pelican said. "Whoa! Take it easy for a minute, young fellow. Take it easy."

Achilles, who was absolutely puffed out, couldn't say a word.

"Well, that was splendid," the pelican said. "Everything went with a glorious bang. And my goodness, you really can run."

"Is anybody—is anybody—is—anybody—following us?"

"Not a sausage."

Achilles panted that he was terribly glad and Popo said:

"Now I'll tell you where we're going. It's only a little further now. There's a very, very nice family in the next village and I happen to know that you're just the young fellow they're looking for."

"Me? How do you know they'll take me?"

"They'll take you. I did them a rather good turn once. They'll do anything for me."

Achilles, who could still hardly believe that all this was happening to him, said:

"But will they beat me? I don't want to be just a beast of burden. I don't hold with it. I've got my feelings, just like anybody else."

"Young fellow," the pelican said, "they'll treat you just like one of the family. When they have carrots you'll have carrots. When they have—"

"Carrots!" Achilles whispered with joy. "Carrots! —"

Suddenly the pelican flew into the air again and Achilles, in a state of blissful happiness, trotted on behind.

In less than half an hour he was standing in a farmyard. Quite a lot of red and white hens were pecking about. A few sheep were resting under a big mulberry tree. A goat was eating some leaves and a pig lay snoring close beside.

But what attracted Achilles most was a young farmer in a

big yellow straw hat and his nice-looking wife in a strawberry-pink dress and a pink-spotted kerchief tied round her black hair and their three young children, two boys and a girl.

"I promised to find you a good young donkey," the pelican said. "Well, here he is."

The three children all laughed and clapped and waved their hands.

"Oh! good. He's nice. What's his name?"

"What's your name, young fellow?" Popo the pelican said. "I never asked you."

Achilles opened his mouth as wide as it would go and gave a huge braying laugh.

"Achilles! That's my name. Achilles!"

All the children and the farmer and his wife laughed too and one of the children patted Achilles on the nose.

"Achilles! That's a nice name. I love that."

Achilles gave another loud braying laugh, almost hysterical

with joy, as if the thought of carrots had gone completely to his head.

"And I'll tell you something else," he said. "I'm not called Achilles for nothing. I've been told. You just remember that."

"Do you know?" the farmer said, "I believe we've got a very exceptional donkey here."

"I believe we have," his wife said. "In fact I'm sure we have. Aren't we lucky?"

"And you're not the only ones," Achilles said.

After which everybody, especially Achilles, was very, very, very happy.